W9-BMF-253

CONTENTS

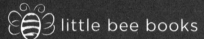 little bee books

251 Park Avenue South, New York, NY 10010
Copyright © 2019 by Little Bee Books
All rights reserved, including the right of
reproduction in whole or in part in any form.
Manufactured in China TPL 0519
ISBN: 978-1-4998-0855-1 (pbk)
First Edition 10 9 8 7 6 5 4 3 2 1
ISBN: 978-1-4998-0856-8 (hc)
First Edition 10 9 8 7 6 5 4 3 2 1

Library of Congress Cataloging-in-Publication Data
Names: Mae, Jamie, author. | Hartas, Freya, illustrator.
Title: The candy cane culprit / Jamie Mae; Freya Hartas.
Description: First edition. | New York, NY: Little Bee Books, [2019]
Series: Isle of Misfits; 4 | Summary: Mythical creatures Gibbon,
Alistair, Ebony, Yuri, and Fiona travel to the North Pole on a mission
to discover who is responsible for vandalizing Santa's toy factory,
putting him behind schedule for Christmas.
Identifiers: LCCN 2019010975 | Subjects: | CYAC: Yeti—Fiction. |
Animals, Mythical—Fiction. | Santa Claus—Fiction. | Christmas—Fiction.
Classification: LCC PZ7.1.M29 Can 2019 | DDC [Fic]—dc23
LC record available at https://lccn.loc.gov/2019010975

littlebeebooks.com

CHAPTER ONE

THE LEGEND OF SANTA

"It's nearing that time of year again!" Mrs. Masry declared cheerfully.

Gibbon perked up at his desk and focused on his teacher, Mrs. Masry. She was a sphinx with the head of a human and the body of lion, so it was hard to miss her as she walked around the room.

"Since Christmas is around the corner, I thought today's lesson should be on creatures and mythology surrounding the holiday." She clicked her slider and an image of an old lady on a broomstick appeared. "In Italy, this is called *La Befana*. Much like Santa Claus, she flies around rewarding good children with gifts and candy, while bad children get coal. Though humans might not believe so, *La Befana* is not really different from a normal witch. This was just something she did to help Santa out before people started noticing her flying around on a broomstick and panicked!"

With another click, her slider changed to reveal a big, hairy creature with wicked horns. Gibbon cringed—whatever that creature was looked so mean, he never wanted to meet one.

"This is a much more well-known creature from Germany, the Krampus. To date, a Krampus has not been found, but legend has it—"

The door to the classroom opened, cutting Mrs. Masry off.

Fitzgerald poked his head into the room. "Hello, Mrs. Masry. Would it be alright with you if I borrowed Gibbon and Alistair?"

"Of course!" Mrs. Masry replied brightly. "Go ahead, boys."

Alistair and Gibbon glanced at each other nervously as they got up. Gibbon didn't think they'd done anything wrong lately.

Ebony, Yuri, and Fiona were already in the hallway. When Gibbon saw them, excitement built up in his chest like a burst of bats. This wasn't about being in trouble, this was about a mission!

Isle of MISFITS

THE CANDY CANE CULPRIT

by JAMIE MAE

illustrated by FREYA HARTAS

little bee books

"What's going on? I'm missing class!" Ebony said anxiously.

"Your team has been making quite a stir lately," Fitzgerald began. "Declan and Cyrus were very pleased with your work and talked you up to all their friends. Word got around, and a very special someone has requested your help."

"Really?" Fiona said with wide eyes.

"Yeah!" Yuri cheered, high-fiving Alistair—or at least, he tried. Alistair missed Yuri's hand and almost fell forward, but Yuri caught him so he didn't hit the ground.

"Who?" Gibbon asked.

"This is a very high priority, very top secret mission," Fitzgerald whispered as he looked around the hallway. "I can't talk about the specifics here. Word cannot get  out about this trouble, or it would cause a panic."

A panic? Top secret mission? A very important someone requesting their help? Gibbon bounced with excitement. This mission was going to be something special!

"I brought you some essentials for this mission. Be sure to bundle up!" Fitzgerald picked up a box from alongside the wall and put it down in front of them.

Gibbon rushed to open the box first. With a raised eyebrow, he pulled out a fluffy sweater with a big, glittery Christmas tree. A bell hung off the sweater at the top of the tree, so it jingled every time it moved.

"We have to wear this?" Yuri asked, taking the sweater from Gibbon.

"It's going to be cold where you're going," Fitzgerald said. "Chop, chop. The quicker you layer up, the quicker we can leave."

Yuri put on the jingly sweater as Fiona pulled out a tiny pair of red-checkered mittens and matching earmuffs. Ebony picked out a green, fluffy hat to protect her ears and a matching scarf. Alistair grabbed the other big sweater, which was decorated with a cat popping out of a present as it ate a gingerbread man. When he pulled it over his head, the pointed scales on his back poked through the fabric. His claws tore the tips of his mittens, too.

8

Gibbon grabbed the last item, a puffy,
oversized candy cane-decorated jacket.

Fitzgerald chuckled and said, "Let's go!"

CHAPTER TWO

A VERY SPECIAL VIP

An icy wilderness greeted them when they landed. Even Fitzgerald shivered in the chilly wind. In the distance, they could see mountains made of nothing but snow and ice. Behind the big wall of ice in front of them, Alistair could see a warm and welcoming glow. But he couldn't figure out what it could possibly be.

Who would they be able to help in a deserted winter wonderland like this? Fiona huddled close to Ebony as both friends' teeth chattered. Yuri seemed perfectly okay, happy even. Alistair wondered if this was the sort of place Yuri used to call home.

"Can we get somewhere warm, *please*? Fairies aren't meant to be this cold!" Fiona said, shivering.

"It shouldn't be much longer," Fitzgerald replied as he searched the sky.

As soon as Alistair took a step forward, he slid on the ice and waved his arms around to try to catch his balance. His clawed feet almost made it seem like he was on ice skates, but there were too many blades to stay stable. Ebony grabbed ahold of his arm and helped him stay upright— just as something zoomed over their heads.

Ebony jumped in surprise as she looked up to see what it was. The sun gleamed so bright in the sky, all she could make out was the creature's outline. What was it? A Pegasus? Hippogriff? No, it didn't look like either of those things—there was more than one flying creature and they were . . . pulling a sleigh?

"Santa!" Fiona shouted with delight. "Hey! It's *Santa*!"

"No way!" insisted Gibbon.

Alistair couldn't believe it! The sleigh circled above before coming down to land right next to them. It kicked up a little snow as it did, but Alistair didn't care. His mouth hung wide open as he watched a big, jolly man in a red suit with a white beard step out of the sleigh.

There was no doubt. It was Santa.

"Ho, ho, ho! Hello, there," Santa greeted them. "You must be the team I've heard so much about! I'm Santa Claus, though some call me Kris Kringle. You can call me Kris. These are my good friends: Dasher, Dancer, Prancer, Vixen, Comet, Cupid, Donner, Blitzen and . . . does he really need any introduction?"

Santa laughed as he patted the lead reindeer on the head, who smiled and raised his red, glowing nose higher.

Santa! Alistair still couldn't believe it. Not just Santa, but Santa *and* his reindeer!

"Fitz, always good to see you." Santa reached out his hand and shook Fitzgerald's.

"Always happy to come visit," Fitzgerald replied.

"Now, let me show you around my workshop." Santa reached into his sleigh and pressed a button. With a shudder, the ice wall opened up to reveal a sprawling village behind it. Alistair realized this was what created the warm glow they had been seeing—a whole town was hidden behind the ice wall! Once they all stepped inside, the cold melted away—like magic!

Alistair could hear Fiona sigh with relief
as she tilted her face toward the glow.

"These are the elves' homes," he explained as they walked past cabins covered in Christmas lights. Elves walked along the icy streets, chatting and nodding hello as they passed by. Some carried grocery bags while others carried tools as they went off to work. At the very center of town was the biggest building of all—a huge factory.

"And here is my factory where all the toys are made." Santa opened a door to the building and let them in. "We only have this one doorway in and out, and all the windows are sealed shut. It helps keep the environment perfect for the elves to paint and craft toys."

"We are so—" Ebony stopped, stumbling over her words as she turned to look up at Santa. "So honored you asked us to help you, Santa, sir!"

"No sirs needed, we're all friends here! You came highly recommended by my good friend Declan. I'm sure you're all wondering why you're here, and I'm afraid to say it's because . . ." For the first time, it looked like Santa's good cheer left him. He frowned as he looked around his factory.

"We've been having a lot of trouble with vandalism in my factory. Worse than just that, toys are being *destroyed*. For the first time ever, we're awfully behind schedule and I'm afraid if we can't get this under control soon . . . we might not have enough toys come Christmas."

CHAPTER THREE

THE MONSTER IN THE MOUNTAINS

*N*ot enough toys for Christmas?!

Gibbon couldn't believe it. Could there be anything worse than that? One Christmas back at the castle, Gibbon had found a lump of coal near the gargoyles' Christmas tree. Surely, it hadn't been meant for him . . . but he never did find out *who* the coal was left for, either. Still, he remembered that crushing moment he saw the coal and thought he wasn't going to get a present. Thankfully, he'd found a wrapped package addressed to him moments afterward.

"Also, *a lot* of candy canes have gone missing, along with some coal," Santa said as he looked down at Gibbon.

Gibbon squirmed and looked away. Thankfully, some elves scurried over to join them.

"We know who the culprit is!" one of the elves said.

Another nodded. "It's the monster of the mountains!"

"Shhh, we shouldn't talk about it," a third elf whispered. "If you talk about it, it will hear you and come for us."

"Oh, hogwash." Santa shook his head. "My elves believe there's some monster that comes down from the mountain and lurks around the North Pole at night. But no one has ever seen it."

"But, Santa!" the elf squeaked. "Even the reindeer are scared!"

"They're always a little anxious around Christmas," a woman said as she walked over to them. She had curly white hair and wore a red dress that matched Santa's suit.

Santa smiled brightly. "Everyone, I would like to introduce you to my wife, Mrs. Claus."

"Fitzgerald! It's been too long," Mrs. Claus declared as she gave the large gargoyle a quick hug. "How about we catch up over a nice cup of hot cocoa and let your students get to work?"

"I'll be around if you need me," Fitzgerald said to the group before following Mrs. Claus across the factory floor.

Once they were gone, Ebony asked, "What do you think is going on here, Santa?"

"I'm not sure, but I do know it's *not* any of my elves. And the ice wall you saw out front circles the whole village. Only the head elf, Mrs. Claus, and myself can open and close the gate, so I don't know how anything could have gotten in."

"A monster sounds pretty bad," Gibbon whispered to Alistair, who nodded in reply.

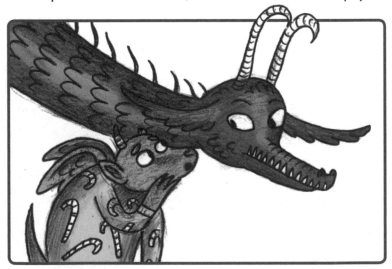

"Psh, I could take it on," Fiona said, throwing punches at an imaginary opponent. "I'll protect you boys, don't worry!"

Santa laughed and waved them along. They walked through the factory where elves were rushing around an assembly line building toys piece by piece. At the very end, an elf grabbed the finished toy and wrapped it up so fast, it made Gibbon stop in awe.

"Come along now," Santa called as he went into the next room. Gibbon rushed to catch up. When he got into the room, his heart jumped in his chest at the sight before him—a room made entirely of candy canes!

The walls were made of it; even the furniture and the pictures were made out of it. It was everywhere!

"You can use this as your headquarters, team," Santa said.

"Kris! We need you out here!" An elf shouted.

"I'll be back in a moment," Santa told them.

After he left, Gibbon walked up to one of the candy cane chairs like he was in a trance. He couldn't hear his friends talking. Every one of his senses was taken up by the candy cane. The delicious, sweet, peppermint-y *candy cane*.

Just one bite, Gibbon thought. It couldn't do any harm if he took just one little, itty, bitty nibble, right? He leaned close to the chair and bit the back of it, sighing with delight at the taste. *Maybe one more . . .*

Before he knew what he was doing, he took one bite, two bites, three, and then more and more!

Once he realized what he'd done, Gibbon covered his mouth with both hands and looked around. His friends gaped at him, their mouths open wide in horror. *Oh, no! I completely ate one of Santa's chairs!*

That had to be naughty-list material!

Santa came back into the room and glanced around, frowning at the area where the chair used to be. "Hmm . . . it looks like even *more* canes are missing now."

CHAPTER FOUR

THE STAKEOUT

Their first night at the factory, the misfits decided to have a stakeout. If the elves were right and there was a monster breaking into the factory, they thought this was the best way to prove it—and maybe even catch it.

Ebony and Yuri were on the east side of the factory, hiding behind some boxes. Alistair and Gibbon were on the west side, crouching beside the present-wrapping table. Since Fiona was the smallest—and the stealthiest—she was flying around in case something showed up.

Fiona wasn't scared one bit. She might be tiny, but she was sure she could take on the creature, no matter its size. She was, however, tired when it finally struck midnight and there was no sign of anything. She sat on top of a table, just about to doze off, when a *CRASH!* came from the south side of the factory. Fiona flew over to Ebony and Yuri, since they were closest to the sound.

"What was that?" Ebony whispered.

"I don't know, we should go check it out," Yuri said.

Then something else shattered right near where the crashing noise came from.

On the other side of the factory, Fiona could see Alistair's shadowy figure ducking beneath the table, barely fitting under it. Gibbon dove down right beside Alistair, covering his head with his hands.

Fiona and Ebony exchanged a look before shaking their heads and following Yuri to the other side of the factory. They were careful not to make any loud sounds themselves. But when they finally got there, all they found were tipped-over boxes and a few broken toys.

"Snow," Yuri whispered as he knelt down and pointed to a half-melted puddle on the ground. Once they picked up the boxes, they found more melting snow underneath. They followed the trail through the factory until they came to where Alistair and Gibbon were hiding. The pair was shaking and holding each other tight.

"Oh, stop being such scaredy-cats," Fiona sighed.

"W-we saw it," Alistair stuttered.

"It ran right by the table!" Gibbon declared. "It was *huge* and had furry feet."

Another *CRASH!* came from somewhere else in the factory. Fiona darted toward the door, since that was the only way for the monster to get out. As she flew, she saw more damaged toys and small chunks of broken candy cane. When she made it to the front door, it was already wide open with no one in sight.

It got away!

CHAPTER FIVE

HOW THE TOYS GET MADE

"I'm just saying, the more candy cane the monster steals, the less candy cane there'll be for everyone else. It's tragic!" Gibbon said with a frown.

"Shouldn't we be more focused on all the toys that were broken last night?" Fiona huffed.

"That's sad, too," Gibbon replied. "But the candy cane . . ."

Alistair patted his friend on the shoulder. Living with Gibbon had taught him a lot about the little gargoyle, including the fact that Gibbon had a mighty strong sweet tooth. "It's okay, buddy. We'll save the toys *and* the candy cane!"

"I think we should split up," Ebony suggested. "Alistair, why don't you stay behind and gather more information about the monster from the elves? Yuri and Fiona, go check the ice mountain and see if you can find anything there. Gibbon, we can search around the North Pole for any way the monster might have gotten past the ice wall."

"Do I have to search outside . . . *where the monster is?*" Gibbon pouted.

"Come on," Ebony urged him as she took his hand.

Alistair was happy to stay in the warm factory and talk with all the elves. Once his friends left, he went from workshop to workshop asking what anyone knew about it. Most were too scared to talk about it until he met Millicent, the head elf. She worked at the very start of the assembly line.

"Oh, *that* monster," Millicent muttered. "It causes us so much trouble!"

"I'm really sorry about that," Alistair said.

"Santa said you'll fix it, and Santa's never wrong," she replied with a curt nod. She paused and looked Alistair over head to toe. "You know, a big guy like you could probably get a *lot* of toys done," she hummed.

"You think so?"

"Wanna give us a hand while you ask your questions?"

"Yes!" Alistair had never made toys before, but he *did* love toys, so he was sure he'd really enjoy making them.

"Okay, here's a set of tools for you." Millicent opened up a box filled with teensy hammers and wrenches and a bunch of other things Alistair didn't know the names of. He swallowed hard. The tools were all so . . . tiny.

His hands? Not so tiny.

"That toy is mostly done," Millicent said as she pointed to a rocking horse. "Could you please bring it over? It usually takes three elves to move those."

Alistair nodded, and it was easy enough. To him, the horse was light and he made sure to take extra care watching his steps as he made his way back to Millicent.

"What do you think the monster is?" Alistair asked as he set the toy down.

"Some say he's the Krampus," Millicent replied. "He's supposed to be a mix between a monster and a man, and very mean. He's the opposite of Santa. It would make sense. We're creating the toys. And he's destroying them."

Alistair nodded as she spoke. *Wasn't Mrs. Masry talking about the Krampus before we left school? She said it's never been found.*

"Now, take the hammer and bang in those nails that are sticking out," Millicent instructed.

Alistair grabbed the horse's head and tried to hit the nails with the tiny hammer, but it was awkward to hold, so he kept missing. As he leaned against the rocking horse trying, trying, and trying again to get those nails  pushed in, he heard a *CRACK!* Jumping away from it, he saw the neck of the horse was dangling forward now.

"I'm sorry!"

"It's okay, we all make mistakes," Millicent said. "Let's give it another go with something else . . . how about that toy robot? Take the screwdriver and finish twisting in the bolts on its back, okay?"

"Santa told us that you're one of the only people who can open the ice wall's gate. Have you seen anything strange near that area whenever you've used it?" Alistair asked as he looked around his box for the screwdriver.

"Nothing that I've ever noticed. It's hard to believe whatever it is would have slipped in that way," Millicent answered as Alistair found the screwdriver. Delicately, he tried to hold it with his claws, but it was hard for him to maneuver. Frustrated, he held the robot a little tighter so it'd stay in place as he tried again when—*CRACK!*

He broke *another* toy. He groaned as he set it down.

"It's okay, it's okay!" Millicent said as she patted his arm. "You didn't mean to, you're a dragon, not an elf. This doesn't come naturally to you."

That made Alistair feel a little better. He was a dragon and this workshop was built for elves, so it made sense he didn't fit in that well.

Wait . . . what if the monster doesn't mean to break things, too? What if he's just too big to get around this tiny workshop like me?

"Why do you think it steals coal?"

Millicent frowned. "I have no idea! Who would *want* coal?"

Alistair stayed with Millicent a little longer, learning her toy-making ways before he started to wander around the workshop again.

He bumped into tables and stubbed his toe on tiny little stools, which made him trip and almost crash into a box of freshly wrapped toys.

The monster really could just be too big! This place is hard for me to walk around in.

Out of the corner of his eye, he saw

something wet on the floor. When he got closer to inspect it, it was clearly footprints leading out the back door, where even more footprints leading away from the building were easy to see in the snow.

Big footprints.

Too big for Santa and his elves or for Ebony and Gibbon.

———— CHAPTER SIX ————

THE NAUGHTY LIST

Ebony shivered as she and Gibbon walked along the ice wall. She couldn't see any way the monster might have been able to get in. Unless the monster could jump really high or maybe fly.

Once they reached the front door, something caught her attention in the snow. She squatted down and picked up a clump of white hair.

"Santa's?" Gibbon asked as he looked over the possible clue.

"This is more . . . fur-like than Santa's hair, don't you think?" Ebony replied.

Gibbon looked closer and nodded. He walked around searching for more, but every time he heard the jingle of reindeer bells or footsteps, he jumped.

"Why are you so anxious, Gibbon? You seemed scared of Santa back in the workshop, too."

Gibbon lowered his head and dug his toes into the snow. "Um, no reason . . ."

"Oh, come on. You can tell me. We're friends!"

Slowly, Gibbon looked up at her. His eyes darted around, making sure no one else was nearby, then he whispered, "I . . . I think I'm on the naughty list."

"You?" Ebony gasped. "I don't believe it. No way, no how."

Gibbon wasn't convinced. "Back at the castle, I could never sit still like I was supposed to, and I played pranks on people. Nothing too bad, mostly just dropping snowballs down on them or moving around into different poses to confuse people. But still . . . I wasn't supposed to do that stuff. It's why Fitzgerald brought me to the isle."

"But since you arrived, you've done nothing but help others. There's no way Santa has you on the naughty list."

Gibbon was about to smile when Alistair appeared around the corner. He was hunched over, looking closely at the ground and walking so fast, he was about to run into them!

"Alistair!" Ebony called out. He looked up and skidded to a stop, kicking up some snow on his friends.

"Oh, hi! What are you guys doing here?" Alistair asked.

"Looking for a way the monster might have gotten in. Look at what we found," Ebony said as she held up the white fur. "I think it might be a clue. What are you doing here?"

"Following these," Alistair said, pointing down to the footprints. "They led me here."

"So they went through the village, and not along the wall," Ebony noted. That had to be why she and Gibbon hadn't noticed them yet.

"The footprints look like they go directly out the gate. We should follow them," Ebony said. She used the key Santa gave her to open the gate. Once they started following the footprints farther and farther away from the ice wall, they came across Yuri's as well.

Hmm, *it's strange how much they look alike*, Ebony thought.

Both sets of footprints were headed toward . . . the mountain!

"Yuri and Fiona went up the mountain, right?" Gibbon gulped.

"And the footprints are going that way, too," Alistair added.

"We have to warn them!" Ebony shouted.

CHAPTER SEVEN

UP IN THE MOUNTAINS

Yuri watched as Fiona shivered more and more the longer they were outside.

"It's too bad you don't have warm fur like me," he said.

"I am beautiful the way I am," Fiona said as she held her head up high. "I'm just not meant for c-cold we-weather."

She wrapped her arms tightly around herself, but almost flew backward when a strong gust of wind hit them. Yuri reached out and let her rest in his hand. She huffed, glaring at him like her poor, furless skin was his fault.

Fiona hummed as she looked him over. "Can I bundle up in your man bun to stay warm? That way, I don't have to worry about flying in this harsh, cold wind, too."

"Sure?" Yuri said a bit uneasily.

Fiona flew up to his head. He could feel her digging her way into his man bun and sighing contentedly once she was seated on his head. "Okay, maybe having fur isn't so bad."

Yuri laughed as they continued up the mountainside. He was built perfectly for this weather and for easily scaling mountains and conquering icy grounds, too. While he didn't come from the North Pole, his home wasn't all too different from here.

"This place is perfect," Yuri said. "If I wanted to, I could sneak around here so easily since I'm all white like the snow. Back home, my brothers and I always did that to play tricks on each other."

As soon as he said it, he realized what it could mean. If no one ever saw the monster during the day . . . maybe it wasn't because it *only* came out at night, but because it was white and blended into the snow, too.

Once they were halfway up the mountain, Fiona pointed out an alcove off to their left.

Yuri walked over to explore it. Inside was a camp with a firepit in the center, a couple crate boxes sitting around like chairs, a unicorn beanie bag, a big stack of picture books, and calendars scattered around that contained pictures of warm places. A book was left open next to the firepit called *How to Blend in With the Locals* that had highlight marks and sticky notes in it.

"Candy cane!" Fiona shouted.

Yuri squatted down and saw little pieces of it everywhere, right next to a comb with lots of white fur and gel caught in it.

"Hey, look over there. What's that?" Fiona asked, pointing to the far side of the camp. Yuri carefully stepped over the firepit and over to an old, brown sleigh filled with pillows and sheets with bunnies on them.

"Looks like someone's bed," Yuri said. But it was a very lumpy one, so Yuri moved the sheets to get a better look only to discover a whole pile of coal.

"Ah-ha! We found our culprit!" Fiona shimmied on his head in excitement.

"Maybe, but this doesn't look like the home of a monster," Yuri said as he glanced over the camp, catching sight of a big stuffed animal that looked well-used. It took Yuri a moment to realize it was a dog, and almost life-sized, too.

Then the sound of footsteps caught his attention. He turned around, seeing a long, dark shadow in the entrance of the alcove.

"It's the monster!" Fiona yelled. "Don't worry, Yuri, I'll protect you!"

The shadow turned into something a little bigger than Yuri, with just as much long, white hair that mostly covered its face. It was another yeti! He danced as he walked, giggling to himself as he held one fistful of candy canes in one hand and cradled a bunch of coal with his other.

Candy cane bits stuck to the fur that hung over his face, and the red of the candy had dyed his fur in other places, too.

Yep, they definitely found their culprit. Except, he wasn't a monster at all.

When the other yeti noticed them, he yelped and dropped everything like he was the one scared. "Wh-wh-who are you?!"

"We're helping Santa. He wanted to know what's been breaking into his factory, destroying toys, and stealing candy cane and coal. It seems like that creature is you!" Fiona said, pointing at the yeti. Instantly, she shivered and pulled her hand back into Yuri's warm fur.

Another shadow rounded the corner of the alcove right before Alistair appeared. He ran straight over to the other yeti, breathing heavily as he did.

"Yuri!" Alistair shouted. "Watch out! The monster is coming this way!"

Ebony and Gibbon rounded the corner next, each eyeing Alistair strangely before looking over to Yuri and Fiona.

"Uh . . . Alistair?" Yuri called out.

His dragon friend jumped as he turned around. "Yuri! Wait, how are you . . . ?" He glanced behind him at the other yeti, then back at Yuri, then back at the yeti again.

"*Ahhhh!*" Alistair stumbled away from the other yeti. After a few clumsy steps, he fell straight into a pile of snow.

"It's okay, Alistair. He's a yeti, like me, and *he's* the one that's been breaking into Santa's shop," Yuri explained. "I just don't know why yet."

The yeti sighed and hung his head low. "I'm sorry! I'm Gunderson. I only went into the workshop to get some coal for my fire. Even us yetis get cold at night."

"Why break all the toys?" Ebony asked.

"I didn't mean to! Everything is so small, and I'm not small at all! I always go when it's dark, because I don't want to scare the little elves. At night, I can barely see. Even during the day, it can be hard because of this long hair!"

"Here," Yuri said as he walked over to his fellow yeti. "Try this!"

Yuri always carried an extra hair tie on his wrist, and being an expert at this by now, he got all of Gunderson's hair up into a bun on the top of his head and tied it in place.

"Wow! Thank you. I can see so much better now!"

"What about the candy canes?" Gibbon asked.

"I know I *shouldn't* take them because they're not mine, but I can't help myself. They're just so delicious!" Gunderson replied nervously.

Gibbon nodded sympathetically. "Yeah, they *are* really good."

"With all the toys you broke, there might not be enough for all the kids at Christmas this year," Alistair said with a frown.

"No!" Gunderson roared, making the mountain shake. All of the misfits shrank back, surprised by the loud cry.

"I didn't mean for that to happen! Is there anything I can do to help Santa and the elves? Please, please, *please*?! I don't want to be the reason someone doesn't get their toys—or worse, their candy canes!"

"Let's go back to the factory and see if there's any way we can help Santa," Ebony suggested.

"Oh, man. Does this mean I'm on the naughty list now?" Gunderson asked, biting his nails.

CHAPTER EIGHT

SAVING CHRISTMAS

"C'mon, guys. We can do this!" Alistair declared as he held up some half-finished toys. "Millicent already taught me how, so I can show you guys, too!"

Ebony and Fiona grabbed their own boxes of tools and sat down next to Alistair. Both quickly caught on, especially Fiona since her tiny hands worked so well with the elves' tools. Yuri and Gunderson, like Alistair, were too big for the tools, but they helped the elves move the heavy bags of toys around the workshop and onto the sleigh.

Gibbon learned he had a knack for wrapping gifts, since his claws worked to not only cut the wrapping paper, but also make the ribbons all pretty and twisty! It took them all day and a lot of effort, but they were able to get all the toys finished.

"We did it!" Millicent cheered at the front of the factory. "We've made all the toys on our list!"

"Indeed, you all did a great job," Santa said, but his smile wasn't as big as Gibbon expected it to be.

"What's wrong?" Fiona asked.

"I'm afraid it still took longer than we expected. I'm hours behind schedule and I'm not sure if I'll be able to deliver all the toys in time. . . . That is, unless I can find someone to help me."

"Help?" Gibbon grinned and looked to his friends, each of them jumping with excitement. Did that mean . . . they could actually go out and deliver toys with Santa? Gibbon couldn't even imagine how cool it would be to ride in the sleigh, shimmy down chimneys, and leave toys under Christmas trees. And all the cookies he would get to eat, too!

"Fitzgerald!" Gibbon turned around to look at the bigger gargoyle, who was enjoying a nice cup of hot cocoa with Mrs. Claus nearby. "Can we? Can we please?"

Fitzgerald took a long sip of his cocoa before putting his mug down. "You've done a great job, so . . . I think you should finish what you started and see this mission through."

Everyone cheered. Ebony flapped her wings in joy while Yuri and Alistair high-fived—successfully this time! And Fiona did a little dance in the air.

Santa placed a red hat on top of Gibbon's head and grinned down at him. "You are all most certainly on my nice list this year."

Gibbon's heart felt like it could soar right out of his chest. He wasn't on the naughty list after all!

"Come along now, we don't have any time to waste!" Santa hopped onto his fully packed sleigh and patted the seat next to him. Giddily, Gibbon scurried into the sleigh and sat down next to Santa. Fiona sat on her friend's shoulder while Gunderson and Yuri made themselves nice and comfy right behind them.

As they took off into the snowy night sky, Ebony and Alistair flew right alongside them, claws clasped, smiling and laughing all the way.

JAMIE MAE is a children's book author living in Brooklyn with her fluffy dog, Boo. Before calling New York home, she lived in Quebec, Australia, and France. She loves learning about monsters, mysteries, and mythologies from all around the globe.

←——————→

FREYA HARTAS is a UK-based illustrator specializing in children's books. She lives in the vibrant city of Bristol and works from her cozy, cluttered desk. Freya loves to conjure up humorous characters, animals, and monsters and to create fantastical worlds and places for them to inhabit and get lost in.

THE
ALIEN
NEXT DOOR

THE
NEW
KID

BY A. I. NEWTON   ILLUSTRATED BY ANJAN SARKAR   1

THE NEW SCHOOL

THE NEW KID SAT ALONE in the back of the bus. He was on his way to his first day at a new school.

Once again.

He watched as the other kids fooled around. They giggled and yelled. No one else seemed to be just sitting in their seat.

Except him. The new kid.

Once again.

Taking this "bus" thing to school with everyone else is really dumb, he thought. *Back home we got to school on our own. And much faster than in this clunky yellow hunk of metal. And instead of messing around the whole way like these kids, we had time to think and prepare for learning. But this . . .*

The new kid shook his head. No one on the bus seemed to even notice that he was there.

Here we go again, he thought. *Will anyone like me? Will I make any friends? Why do my parents have to move so much?*

The new boy sighed. He knew why they were always moving. They were research scientists. Their work took them from place to place. And every time they moved, he had to start over in a new school. He had to make new friends. He had to learn how things were done in a new place.

"Hey, Charlie!" one kid shouted at his friend. "Did you finish last week's homework?"

"I finished it this morning," another kid shouted back. "Right on time!"

The bus rocked with laughter.

The new kid didn't understand. What was funny about waiting until the last minute to do your schoolwork? He didn't like always feeling different. He was tired of being the strange new kid once again.

And he missed his home.

I have friends back home. I know how stuff works there. All of this is so . . . different, so strange.

The bus slowed to a stop and the doors opened. The kids bounded down the stairs and ran toward the school.

The new kid got out of his seat. He walked slowly to the front of the bus to exit.

"Good luck today," said the bus driver. She smiled warmly at him. It made him feel a little better.

Here I go again, he thought. Then he took a deep breath, walked into the school, and hoped for the best.

Journey to some magical places and outer space, rock out, and find your inner superhero with these other chapter book series from **Little Bee Books!**

little bee books

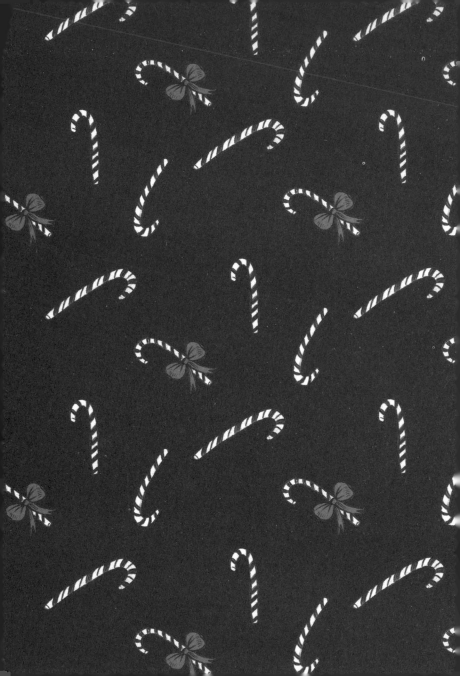